60

Three ...bums!

Eleven **#1** hits on CHOMP FM!

PUT YOUR FINS TOGETHER FOR...

First published by Albert Street Books, an imprint of Allen & Unwin, in 2024

Allen & Unwin
Cammeraygal Country
83 Alexander Street
Crows Nest NSW 2065
Australia
Phone: (61 2) 8425 0100
Email: info@allenandunwin.com
Web: www.allenandunwin.com

*Allen & Unwin acknowledges the Traditional Owners of the Country
on which we live and work. We pay our respects to all Aboriginal and
Torres Strait Islander Elders, past and present.*

 A catalogue record for this
book is available from the
National Library of Australia

ISBN 978 1 76118 110 8

For teaching resources, explore allenandunwin.com/learn

Cover design by Yell Design and Allen & Unwin design team
Text design and typesetting by Rebecca Timmis, Hannah Janzen
and Allen & Unwin design team
Set in 16 pt Queulat Cnd Soft
Printed and bound by CPI Group (UK) Ltd, Croydon, CR0 4YY

10 9 8 7 6 5 4 3 2 1

www.rjtimmis.net

JAWSOME
Licence to Rock

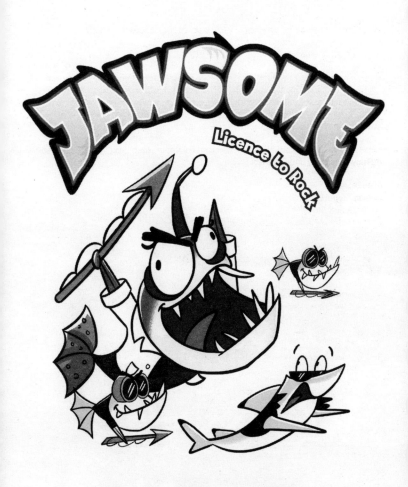

R.J. Timmis

ALBERT STREET BOOKS

Licence to Rock

Chapter One

Well, hey there!

I'm Finley – super-normal shark kid by day, totally famous **rock star** by night.

This is my band, **JAWSOME**. The other three members are my best friends **Hunter, Gilleon** and **Gnash**.

HUNTER
Harriet Heartfins

GILLEON
Grayson Glitter

GNASH
Gnarly Gnelson

But then, you probably already know all this, right? Everyone's heard of **JAWSOME**. We're as famous as the **Statue of Flipperty**. And **Buckingfin Palace**. And even the **Offal Tower**.

Today we're heading off to **Euro-fishin!** It's all the way across the ocean in **Shell-bania**. I've already packed my suitcase.

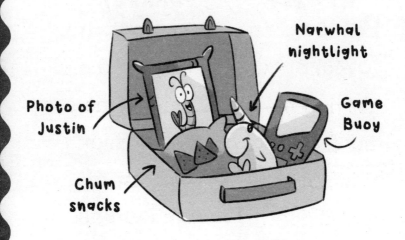

Photo of Justin

Narwhal nightlight

Game Buoy

Chum snacks

And said goodbye to my pet prawn, Justin.

I've even made a head start on my history homework.

Right now, Mum and Dad are driving me to the submarine port. My friends and I will be taking Jawsome's **private sub** to Shell-bania. I'm nervous and excited as we approach the subport. International concerts are so much fun! Even though we'll be competing against bands from other oceans, we also get to stay up late and party with shell-ebrities like **Swim Shady** and **Mer-tallica**. There will be TV interviews and selfies with fans, and there's always...

SO MUCH FOOD!

I tug my big hat down around my sunglasses as we make our way through the terminal. If anyone recognises me, it will create a **riot!** Hugo, our band manager, is waiting for us by the gift shop. Today he's pretending to be our teacher.

← FOOD COURT
GATE 42 →

Super Normal
School Excursion
Meet-up Point

Gilleon and Hunter are already there, gleefully clutching their suitcases.

'Bye, Mum! Bye, Dad!' I kiss my parents on their cheeks and scoot over to Hugo.

Mum and Dad swim off, waving back at me one last time. We tour so often, they don't even cry at the subport anymore.

Hugo takes my suitcase. Hunter, Gilleon and I hover around, chatting excitedly about the competition. Everything from our performance to our costumes are totes **OUT OF THIS WORLD!**

Hugo keeps glancing at his watch. The minutes tick by.

Then a whole hour.

Hugo scratches his chin.
'I'd better call Gnash's parents,' he says. He pulls out his shell-phone and swims to a quiet corner, careful to keep an eye on us.

After a few minutes, he comes back. His eyes are wide and his flippers are shaking. 'Kids, I have some **bad news,**' he says.

Hunter, Gilleon and I swap a worried look.

'Did Gnash get lost?' asks Hunter.

'Or stuck in the bath again?' asks Gill.

I gasp. 'Is he sick? I *tried* to tell him not to eat the sandpit at school.'

'Worse,' says Hugo. 'I just spoke to Mr and Mrs Pointer. Gnarly Gnelson is

OFFICIALLY MISSING.'

Chapter Two

Hugo is in **total panic mode.**

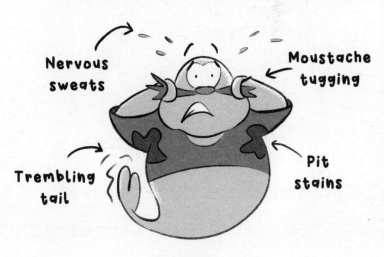

Nervous sweats

Moustache tugging

Trembling tail

Pit stains

'B-b-but what about **Euro-fishin?**' I squeak. 'We can't do it without Gnash!'

'You mean I dyed my fringe for nothing?' wails Gill. Gilleon's fringe is a total icon; it's in the **Fin-nes World Records** and everything:

'I dunno,' says Hunter, looking unconvinced. 'Are we sure Gnash didn't just get lost on the way to the toilet or something?'

I shake my head. Gnash might not be so good with directions. Or doors labelled **Push** and **Pull**. Or following instructions like **don't eat the sandpit**. But he's never missed a show, *ever*. 'No way,' I say. 'Something fishy is going on. Gnash wouldn't let us down like this.'

'You're right, Finley,' says Hugo. 'This is serious. Poor Mr and Mrs Pointer are **beside themselves.**'

'Beside themselves?' I ask, scratching my head. 'Like on the couch?'

'It means they're **upset,**' Hunter explains. Along with having good (and bad) ideas, Hunter is super smart. She was even chess champion at school...until she ate all the chess pieces (tiger sharks will eat **ANYTHING**).

'The contest starts in two days,' says Hugo. 'That gives us forty-eight hours to find Gnash and get you all to **Shell-bania**.'

'Then what are we waiting for?' says Gilleon. 'Let's go!'

We squish into Hugo's sub and zoom over to Gnash's house on **Deep Side**.

putt-putt-putt...

SUBPORT

'See?' I whisper to Hunter as we swim inside. 'Gnash's parents **are** beside themselves.'

Hugo tries to console Mr and Mrs Pointer. 'Can you tell me what happened?' he asks gently.

Mrs Pointer dabs her eye with a tissue. 'Gn-Gn-Gnash was packing his suitcase upstairs,' she says. 'I went to make him a chum sandwich, and when I came back, he was **g-g-gone!**'

'Have you called the police?' asks Hugo.

'W-w-we can't,' wails Mr Pointer. 'We're **too upset!**'

'There, there,' says Hugo, patting Mr Pointer on the back so hard his false teeth **fly out**. 'Leave it to me.'

Hugo whips out his shell-phone and calls triple zero. 'Hello? Police? This is Hugo Hefty, band manager for **JAWSOME**. Our drummer, **Gnarly Gnelson,** is missing!'

There's
a crackly
voice on
the other
end.

'What?'
bellows
Hugo. 'This
isn't a hoax!
**Gnarly
Gnelson** is *really missing!*'

More crackles.

'Wasting your time? Right!
That's it!' Then he uses some
words that aren't allowed in kid's
books and hangs up.

Mr and Mrs Pointer cry even harder. Hugo barrels off to make them a cup of **chum-o-mile** tea.

'Come on,' says Hunter, edging her way towards the stairs. 'Let's go check out Gnash's room.'

'What for?' I ask.

'To look for clues, of course,' says Hunter. 'If we want to find Gnash, we're going to have to do it **ourselves.**'

Chapter Three

Upstairs, it's exactly like Mrs Pointer said. Gnash's suitcase is open on the bed. Inside it is his teddy bear, a giant toothbrush (Gnash's teeth are **shark-normous**) and his favourite bandana.

Gnash's toothbrush →

← Regular toothbrush

Hunter checks the window. 'No sign of a break-in,' she says.

'No clues in the wardrobe,' I say.

'Nothing under the bed,' says Gilleon. 'Except for this ancient slice of **chum-and-pineapple pizza,**' he adds, sticking out his tongue.

'Dibs!' cries Hunter. She plucks the pizza slice from Gill and throws it down her gullet. 'Mmm, extra mould. My **favourite.**'

Gill and I try not to gag.

'This is so weird,' I say, looking around. 'Sharks don't just vanish. Especially ones the size of Gnash.'

We keep searching, looking in drawers, under the rug, even inside the tank belonging to Sheldon, Gnash's pet hermit crab.

Then Hunter narrows her eyes, sniffing the water. 'Hey, do you guys smell that? It's like... **fish guts and vanilla.**'

Gilleon makes a face. 'Ew. That's almost as bad as pairing stripes and spots.'

'Maybe it has something to do with this?' I say, picking up something sticking out from under Gnash's suitcase. It's a business card. Hunter and Gilleon sail over to see.

'F.I.S.H.? What's that?' asks
Hunter.

'Never heard of it,' I say. 'Maybe
there's something on the back?'

I turn the card over. On the other side is a **symbol**.

'Hmm,' says Gill, 'I think I've seen that symbol before...'

'To the **finternet?**' suggests Hunter.

Gill grins. 'To the **finternet!**'

Chapter Four

We zoom over to Gnash's desk and switch on his laptop. Gilleon snaps a shot of the symbol on his shell-phone, uploads it to the laptop and runs an image search.

- Ping!

One result pops up: a **blurry photo** of a billboard.

'Dull Street?' sniffs Gilleon. 'Sounds **otterly boring**.'

'Wait a second,' says Hunter, leaning closer to the screen. 'Those buildings in the background look like the **Business District**.'

'Then let's go!' I cry. 'Maybe Hugo can give us a ride?'

We all swim downstairs. In the living room, Mr and Mrs Pointer are still on the couch, sobbing.

Hugo is on the phone again. 'Hello, famous news reporter **Barry Mundy?**' he shouts.

'I have a story I need you to break. Gnarly Gnelson from **Jawsome** is missing!

We need everyone searching for him right now – police, private finvestigators, dogfish walkers – everyone! What? No, this isn't a **prank call**. I'm his band manager, Hugo Hefty. Whaddya mean,

never heard of me?!'

'Um, looks like Hugo has his **flippers full,**' says Hunter.

'Maybe we should leave him here.'

'Good idea,' says Gilleon.

'Besides, riding in his mini sub does nothing for my street cred.'

We sneakily sail out the door and hop on a bus to the **Business District.** Ten minutes later we arrive on Dull Street. Hunter, Gilleon and I spot the billboard with the **F.I.S.H. symbol**. It's in front of the ocean's most boring-looking building.

'There's something **weird** about

WELCOME TO
DULL STREET
where nothing ever happens

this place,' says Hunter. 'Look –
there's no door. And the windows
are made of **tinfoil**.'

We swim up to the building and check. She's right.

'What kind of building has **no door?**' I wonder aloud.

'And **fake windows?**' says Gill.

'A building you don't want anyone to get into,' answers Hunter. 'Or *see* into. There's definitely something **sea-spicious** going on here.'

Gill sighs at his reflection in the tinfoil. 'We need to get inside – this humidity is terrible for my fringe!' he says. 'Maybe there's a back door. Or a way in from the roof. Or–'

'Or we could just follow **those guys?**' I say.

Hunter and Gilleon turn around.
A line of sharks in dark suits
are waiting outside an old-timey
phone box next to the building.
One by one they swim into the
box and then **WHOOSH,** they
disappear.

'I don't know much about **ancient tech,**' says Gill, 'but I'm pretty sure that's not how phone boxes work.'

The last shark in line gets swallowed up. 'Come on,' says Hunter with a wide grin. 'Let's **check it out.**'

Chapter Five

We look around to
make sure
no one is
watching.
Then we sidle
over to the
phone box and
peek inside.

'What's that curly thing?' I ask, pointing at the phone. 'A **tail?**'

'And where's the **screen?**' asks Gilleon.

'And why's it so **big?**' asks Hunter.

Old-timey things are **weird**.

We all squish inside the box.

'What now?' says Gill.

'Try picking up the phone,' says Hunter.

I'm the closest, so I pick the receiver up and hold it to my ear. A strange beeping sound screeches out. 'I think it's **broken,**' I say.

'Hmm,' says Hunter, whipping out the business card we found in Gnash's room. 'There's something written under Agent Chip's name. Try entering the code **4-2-1-1**.'

I stare at the phone. 'Er – how do I do that?'

'Press the numbers in those little circles?' suggests Hunter. I try that. **Nothing happens.**

'I think I saw one of these phones on **ChewTube** once,' says Gilleon. 'Let me try.'

For each number in the code, he sticks his fin in the little number hole, twists it around to the stop, then lets go.

Bzzzz, click, a-tikka-tikka-tikka.
Bzzzz, click, a-tikka-tikka-tikka.

Once the code has been put in,
I put the phone back to my ear.

'Someone's talking!' I gasp.
'Hello? This is Finley. We're
looking for our friend Gnash.'

A woman's voice answers.
'Good morning, agent. Prepare to
enter the **suction chamber.'**

'The *what*?' I say,
alarmed. 'No, no,
I said we're looking
for **Gnash**–'

'Keep your fins at your sides at all times,' says the voice. 'Flash photography is strictly forbidden. Have a safe trip!'

'But I–' Uh-oh. I don't think I'm talking to an actual shark.

'It's a recording!' I say to Gilleon and Hunter.

'Quick! It's going to...'

Before I can warn them, the bottom of the phone box slides open and we get sucked underground.

WHOOSH!

We zoom through an underground tunnel. It twists and turns and loop-the-loops.

'AAAUGH!' I scream.

'Do *all* phone boxes do this?' cries Gilleon.

'I hope so!' yells Hunter. She throws her fins up and squeals with delight. 'Sharks in the olden days were **FUN!**'

We reach the end of the tunnel
and shoot out into a strange room.
On the walls are giant screens
with maps and codes and photos
of mean-looking **anglerfish**.

Below the screens are sharks
in suits hovering over computers.
On the wall is a big sign reading
F.I.S.H. HEADQUARTERS.

The sharks all stare up at us
with their jaws hanging open.

'Um,' I say, looking at the sharks
in suits. I hold up the business card
we found in Gnash's bedroom. 'So...
anyone here named **Agent Chip?**'

Chapter Six

The three of us stare at the sharks in the suits.

The sharks in the suits **stare back**.

Then lots of things happen at once:

1. Metal doors snap shut over all the exits.

2. Red lights start flashing.

3. The sharks in suits surround us.

A pair of **extra-large** sharks loom over us. 'My name is **Secret Agent Con**,' says one of them. She has sharp eyes and a purple mohawk. 'Last name, **Seal**.'

'And I'm **Frond**,' says the other one. '**James Frond**.'

'We're in charge here,' growls Agent Con. 'Now tell us who you work for!'

'Um, H-Hugo?' I stammer.

'Hugo, eh?' says Frond. 'Must be **Sea-I-A. Ocean Defence Department? Finterpol?**'

'Er, he's our band manager,' says Hunter.

'And how'd you get in here?' barks Agent Con.

'Through the tunnel under your old-timey phone box, of course,' says Gilleon.

Agent Con puts her fins on her hips. 'I told you, Agent Frond,' she says to the shark next to her. 'That secret entry is a **dud**. F.I.S.H. should have gone with a **shell-icopter pad** on the roof like I suggested.'

Agent Frond rolls his eyes.

'What's FISH?' asks Gilleon. Then his eyes light up. 'Are you a new chumshake bar? With some kind of retro spy theme? I love those places!'

'We're not a chumshake bar!' cries Agent Frond, throwing up his fins.

'F.I.S.H. stands for **Federal Investigators of Suspicious Hijinks**. We're the top spy agency in the ocean.

And you kids can't simply bust into our HQ **willy-nilly**.'

'P-p-please, Agent Frond,' I plead. 'We're only here because our friend Gnash is missing. We found a clue in his bedroom that led us to this building.' I hold up the F.I.S.H. business card again.

Agent Frond takes a peek at it. 'Ugh, not again.' He turns to the sharks in suits surrounding us. 'Agent Chip, how many times do we have to tell you – don't take your business cards on missions!'

A little pygmy shark up the back raises his hand. 'Sorry, sir!' he yelps. 'Won't happen again, sir!'

'Wait,' I say, 'did you say **mission?**' My heart starts to beat faster. 'So...you must know where Gnash is!'

'Of course,' says Agent Con. 'He's right over there.' She points to the front of the room where important-looking sharks are hovering around something. Or is it... **someone?** They all move aside to reveal...

'*GNASH!*' Hunter, Gilleon and I all shout his name together.

We zoom over and throw our fins around him.

'We found you!' cries Hunter.

'Hunter!' Gnash cries, beaming. 'Finley! Gilleon!'

I look around at the sharks in the dark suits and sunglasses. 'But Gnash...what are you doing here?' I ask.

Gnash gives us all a toothy grin.

'Gnash helping to save world.'

Chapter Seven

'Err...'

Hunter, Gilleon and I swap a look.

Gnash is great. Like, the **best friend** ever. But he's not exactly...

... spy material.

I look around the room. 'Are you making everyone coffee?' I ask.

'Doing the photocopying?' says Hunter.

'Answering the phone?' says Gill.

'Don't be **sea-donk-u-lous!**' says Agent Con. She puts a fin on Gnash's shoulder. 'Gnash here is helping us take down **A.B.B.A.**, the most notorious organisation in the ocean!'

Gilleon gasps. 'You mean the **Alliance of Brutally Bad Anglerfish?**' he squeals. 'They're the number one villains on toptenevildoers.com!'

TOP 10 EVILDOERS

1. A.B.B.A.
2. Shark Vadar
3. Gold Fishfinger
4. Finnibal Lecter
5. Cruella de Gill
6. Jack the Flipper
7. Hans Chewber
8. Shoaldemort
9. Goldfish Freddy
10. Count Chumula

'They sure are,' says Agent Con. 'A.B.B.A. have been sending coded messages to their operatives for weeks. We think they're planning **something big**, but we haven't been able to crack their code.'

'That's where your friend Gnash comes in,' says Agent Frond. 'A.B.B.A.'s code uses a super-advanced **algae-rhythm**.'

'Algae-what?' I ask.

'Oh, I think he means algorithm,' Hunter says. 'It's a set of rules that computers use to solve problems.'

'No, not algorithm,' says Agent Frond. '*Algae-rhythm*. It's a **complex beat** that's almost impossible to decipher. Gnash here happens to have the best rhythm in the entire ocean – he's an algae-rhythm genius!'

'It's really no surprise,' says Agent Con. 'Gnash being a **famous drummer** and all.'

'Wait,' I say. My heart starts beating faster. 'You know that Gnash is really...'

'**Gnarly Gnelson?**' Agent Frond jumps in. 'Of course!'

Hunter, Gilleon and I all gasp. Oh, no! Our secret identities are supposed to be just that – **SECRET!**

'Don't get your fins in a twist,' says Agent Con. 'We have level three thousand clearance – Gnash's secret is safe with us.'

Phew.

'We've been working on this for hours,' says Agent Frond. 'Gnash, why don't you show your friends around HQ? You can end it with the chum buffet.'

We all gasp again, this time with delight.

Our tour of **F.I.S.H. HQ** is **sea-tacular.**

Gnash shows us the spy equipment room, training gym,

surveillance room, and even...

a super secret

shrink ray!

THE SHRINKINATOR

'So, can it shrink my homework?'

'Or a pimple?'

'Wow, Gnash,' I say, giving him an extra hug, 'this is so cool! You're a **real spy!**'

'Naw,' says Gnash, blushing. 'Just love drumming.'

Finally we sail into the break room. Agent Frond wasn't kidding – in the centre of the room is a giant chum buffet.

We dive in, eating up a storm.

There's chum pizza.

Chum nuggets.

Even chum-flavoured ice cream.

Sea-licious!

After we've eaten, we sink to the seabed, our tummies nice and full.

'So, do you think you'll break the code soon?' Hunter asks Gnash as she nibbles on a piece of chum-and-pecan pie. 'If we're not in Shell-bania by tomorrow night, Hugo's going to **blow a tusk!**'

'No problem,' says Gnash with a grin. 'Only need to solve one more beat–'

Suddenly the lights go out.

'EEEK!' cries Gilleon.

'What's going on?'

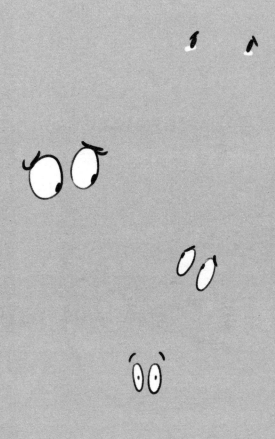

We cling to each other in the dark. The light of a shell-phone flares up beside me. It's Hunter, cool and collected as always. 'It's probably an overloaded circuit board,' she says, heading for the door. 'We better get back to the control room.'

As we head towards the door, voices float down the corridor and into the break room.

'Stage one complete,' someone says. 'We've **breeched the building.**'

The four of us swap a scared look. *Breeched the building?*

'Roger,' replies a second voice. This one sounds like it's coming from a walkie-talkie. 'Operation **EVIL TAKE-DOWN** is underway!'

Chapter Eight

Hunter quickly tucks her shell-phone away as we hide behind the break-room door.

'Operation Evil Take-down?' I whisper. 'That can't be good!'

'It sounds like F.I.S.H. HQ is being **infiltrated!**' says Hunter.

'Infil–*what*?' says Gnash.

'It means broken into,' Hunter explains.

Gilleon peeks around the door. 'Oh, no,' he whispers to us. **'Anglerfish!** That means only one thing...A.B.B.A. are invading F.I.S.H. HQ!'

More A.B.B.A. agents swim past. They're wearing special goggles and carrying...gulp... harpoons!

My fins start to tremble. 'We're trapped,' I squeak. 'How can we get back to the control room without getting harpooned?'

Gnash's eyes light up. 'I know! Use filtration vents.'

Gilleon gasps. 'You mean like John MerClane in **Fry Hard?** I *love* that movie!'

'Good thinking, Gnash,' says Hunter. She turns her shell-phone light on again and swoops it over the ceiling. 'Look! There's a vent right up there.' She sniffs the water a few times. 'And I think I know **exactly** where to go.'

We all swim up to the vent cover in the ceiling. Gilleon prises it off and we duck inside.

'Are you sure you know the way?' I ask Hunter as she takes the lead.

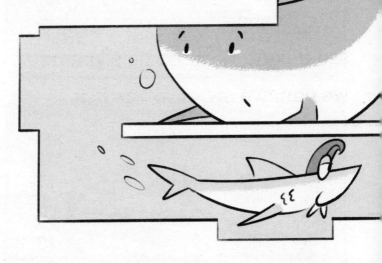

'Of course,' she says, sniffing the water again. 'Remember the **fish guts and vanilla** smell in Gnash's room? Well, let's just say Agent Chip uses way too much cologne. If he's in the control room, I can find it.'

We follow Hunter through so many left turns and right turns, I have **no clue** where we are. Then, a short way up ahead, we see a light. Keeping as silent as we can, we swim towards it.

Bingo!

We've reached the control room!
We peer through the nearest
vent and into the room below.
Things do *not* look good.

THE SHRINKINATOR

'Oh, no!'

I whisper. 'It looks like they're after the shrink ray. Should we call the police?'

'The *fashion police*, maybe,' says Gill. 'Why are they all wearing tinted goggles? They look **sea- diculous**.'

'Hmm,' says Hunter. 'Anglerfish live right down at the bottom of the ocean, where it's super dark. It must be too bright for them up here.'

At that moment an important-looking anglerfish wearing a lab coat bursts into the room.

'Doctor Finrot!' shouts the A.B.B.A. agent by the monitor, giving a salute. 'We've taken control of the **shrink ray** as planned. Everything is ready for you, ma'am.'

Beside me, Gnash gasps. 'Oh, no! Doctor Finrot **super-evil leader** of A.B.B.A.! Agent Frond tell me she once went to movies and not even put ringtone on silent.'

'Wow,' I say, shuddering. 'That **is** evil.'

We watch as Doctor Finrot swims up to the computer below the giant monitor. 'Good work, Agent Bottomfeeder,' she says, then begins typing a code into the computer. A **counter** appears on the screen.

It starts to tick down.
14:59, 14:58, 14:57 . . .

Hunter, Gilleon, Gnash and I all swap terrified looks.

'What happens at zero?' Gill asks. We all shrug.

'You'll never get away with this, Finrot!' shouts Agent Con. 'Stealing access to F.I.S.H.'s secret shrink ray is a **level eighty hundred offence**. You'll be put in jail for a **krillion years!**'

'HA!' yells Doctor Finrot. 'When this counter reaches zero, there won't BE any jails to put me in! There'll be **no jails**, **no sharks**, and **no CHUMVILLE**. And do you want to know WHY?'

The F.I.S.H. agents look at each other warily.

'You're going to **shrink the city?'** suggests Agent Frond tentatively.

'Mwa haa haaa!' laughs Doctor Finrot. 'What a silly idea. No, I have much **grander plans**. We are going to shrink...

...the **SUN.'**

Chapter Nine

We all **stare** at Doctor Finrot in shock.

'Did she just say she's going to **shrink the sun?**' I whisper.

'Our sun?' says Gilleon.

'The sun sun?' Hunter repeats.

'Whose son?' asks Gnash.

'Shhh!' we all say.

'But…but…but…' stammers Agent Frond. 'Without the sun, we can't survive!'

'You mean you can't survive,' says Doctor Finrot. 'Us anglerfish, we **hate** the stupid sun! It's far too big and bright, and it burns our poor sensitive eyes. If we want to take over the surface waters, it simply has to go!'

'Take over the surface?' gasps Agent Con. 'But anglerfish live in deep ocean.'

'Exactly!' cries Doctor Finrot.

'Right down the bottom. Do you have any idea what you surface-dwelling critters do all day? **You POO**. All of you! Octopuses and whales and squid and sea snakes, and don't get me started on all you fish. You just **POO, POO, POO,** all day long. And you know what happens to all that **stinky, slimy POO?**'

'It fertilises the seaweed?' suggests Agent Chip. 'Delivers nutrients to coral reefs?' asks another agent.

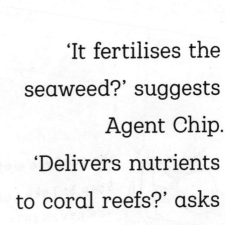

'Uh oh...'

'It **sinks!**' shouts Doctor Finrot. 'All the way down to the **bottom of the sea,** where WE all live. We spend all day swimming around in your POO. It gets in our laundry. Up our nostrils. In our food! Well, we anglerfish have had enough! We want to swim in clean

Step 1: Steal F.I.S.H.'s super secret shrink ray.
Step 2: Shrink the sun so the surface waters turn dark.
Step 3: Take over the ocean and never swim in other fishes' POO ever again!

waters for once. And my krill-iant **three-step plan** is going to ensure our victory. It's otterly **stool-proof!** Er, I mean **FOOL-proof.'**

'You'll never get away with this, Finrot!' shouts Agent Con.

Doctor Finrot gives an evil laugh. 'Hahaha! Really? You have only nine minutes left to stop me, and each and every one of you is tied up. Say goodbye to your **pesky little sun.**'

BWA-HAA-HAA!

Up in the vent, the four of us turn to each other.

'This is a **crab-tastrophe!**' Hunter whispers. 'We have to do something.'

'Like what?' I ask. 'These are the **number-one villains** in the world, remember? We're just ordinary **school** sharks!'

'We're way more than ordinary sharks,' says Hunter. 'We're **JAWSOME**. There's nothing ordinary about us!'

Gilleon puts his snout in the air. 'What are we supposed to do, **sing them a lullaby?'**

'Hmm,' says Hunter. 'Being a rock star isn't just about music. It's also about...**stage presence.'** A toothy grin spreads across her face. 'I think I might have an idea.' She reaches into her jaws and pulls out a backpack.

'What's that?' I ask.

'My carry-on luggage,' she answers simply. 'I always carry it with me.' Then she grins. 'Now, listen up. We're going to

put on a show and **invade** the
invaders!'

Chapter Ten

My tail starts to tingle. We're going to help take down A.B.B.A.?

UNREEL!

'Here's the plan,' says Hunter. 'We're gonna dazzle A.B.B.A. with our sea-sational **Euro-fishin performance**. Then, while they're distracted, we'll kill the countdown and **save the sun!**'

Gill claps his fins together. 'A pop-up performance? I'm totes in!'

Gnash and I nod, grinning – smashing it on stage is what we do best!

EQUIPMENT ROOM ➡

'We have less than **nine minutes** to pull this off,' says Hunter. 'First up, **equipment!**'

'Next…costumes!'

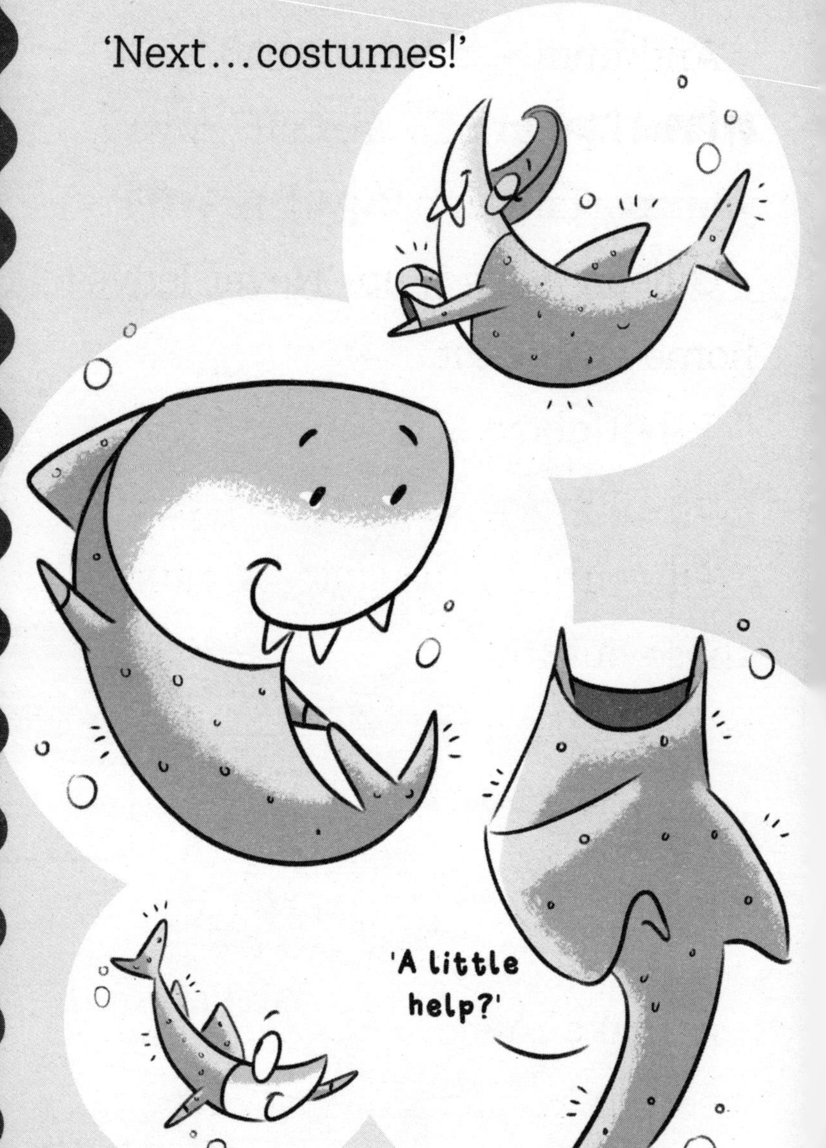

'And finally,' says Hunter, **'atmosphere!** Gill, do you have your portable smoke machine?'

Gilleon holds it up. 'Never leave home without it.'

'What about your emergency stage lights?'

'Of course,' says Gilleon, pulling those out too.

I shake my head in wonder. Gill's always ready to **make an entrance**.

Once everything is set up, we huddle in the vent above the control room.

Hunter rubs her fins together. 'When I give the word, we bust into the control room and put on our best performances,' she whispers.

'A.B.B.A. agents **going down!**' adds Gnash.

My tail shakes nervously.
'Everyone ready?' says Hunter
Gilleon, Gnash and I nod.

'Let's get sneaky!'

She hands lasers to Gnash
and Gilleon. Then she plugs her
shell-phone into the supersonic
spy speakers we borrowed
from the equipment room and
loads up our performance song,
"Fintergalactic".

Gilleon flicks on the smoke
machine and stage lights, while

Gnash prises open the vent cover
that leads to the control room.
Hunter starts up the music.
It blares through the speakers.

'Lights,' says Hunter,
'camera...
ACTION!'

Chapter Eleven

The four of us **DIVE** down into the control room.

Smoke pours down after us. Coloured lights and laser beams flash around the room, while spacey intro music bounces off the walls.

Hunter cups her fins around her mouth and yells, 'Presenting... **Gnarly Gnelson, Harriet Heartfins, Grayson Glitter** aaaand **Felix Frenzy,** of the one and only **JAWSOME!**'

We sail into formation as the song strikes up and I start to sing.

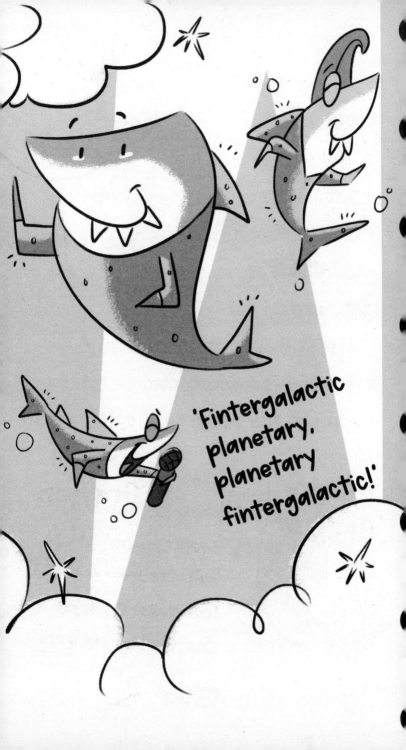

'What the **devilfish** is going on?' cries Doctor Finrot. 'How did **JAWSOME** get here?'

The A.B.B.A. agents all stop what they're doing and watch as I rap out the song.

'Well, I gotta keep swimming, keep swimming full steam. Too sweet to be a shark, too nice to be bream!'

While I do my best robot dance, Hunter, Gilleon and Gnash boogie around the **tied-up agents**. The anglerfish are so mesmerised by my finterstellar dancing, they don't even notice I'm performing solo. As I rap and bust moves, Hunter, Gilleon and Gnash use the **laser pointers** to zap through the agents' bonds. Then they sail back to me, ready for our

grand finale.

'It's time to **INVADE!**' we shout together.

As soon as we sing the last word, the F.I.S.H. agents jump into action, shooting net guns and lasers. Sharks and anglerfish swim in all directions.

It's **CHAOS!**

Doctor Finrot looks around the control room. Seeing the F.I.S.H. agents are free, she turns on her tail and scurries out the door.

'MUMMYYYYYYYYY!' she cries at the top of her gills.

'Quick!' cries Hunter. 'We have to disable the shrink ray!'

The four of us race over to the main computer. Hunter bashes on the keyboard. 'The program's **encoded**. I can't break it!'

Gnash gently pushes her out of the way. 'Gnash can do it.'

Gilleon, Hunter and I watch as Gnash plugs his headphones to the computer. Then he **tippity-taps** away on the keyboard. At first it looks like random tapping, but then we realise... **it's a beat**.

'He's cracking **A.B.B.A.'s algae-rhythm!**' cries Gilleon. 'GO, GNASH!'

Gnash taps. He drums. He **raps his knuckles** and bangs his fists. He even drums with his head!

Then... **PING!**

The countdown stops.

'Gnash!' Hunter, Gilleon and I all cry, squeezing our giant friend in a hug. 'YOU DID IT!'

'Gnash not just like rhythm,' he says, grinning wide. **'Gnash love it.'**

Suddenly the music stops. The flashing lights are cut off, and the smoke disappears.

Agent Con and Agent Frond

glide up to us. 'That was FIN-CREDIBLE!' Agent Con cries. 'You helped defeat A.B.B.A. and disabled the shrink ray. You are some **sea-riously clever rock stars!**'

'How can we ever thank you?' says Agent Frond.

Hunter and I exchange a look. 'All we really want is our friend back,' says Hunter.

Agent Con gives us a wide smile. 'Oh, I think we can do one better than that.'

The next morning, F.I.S.H. awards the four of us with **GOLD CLAMS**, the highest medal in the whole organisation.

Right after the award ceremony Agent Con whisks us off to the subport. She's offered to take us to Shell-bania in a **supersonic F.I.S.H. sub** so we get to the contest on time. **Euro-fishin** will be a piece of chum after what we've just done!

As we board our private sub to Shell-bania, I pull Gnash aside.

'Hey, Gnash?' I say.

'What up, Finley?'

'Um, I'm sorry we all underestimated you,' I say, rubbing my neck. 'You really are one seriously **fin-tastic shark.'**

'Thanks,' says Gnash, beaming brightly. 'Gnash think Finley awesome, too.'

'Naw,' I say, grinning. 'We're **JAWSOME**. And that's **even better**.'

Chapter One

Today is Thursday.

And that means...

REHEARSALS DAY!

135

Hunter, Gilleon, Gnash and I are jamming at **Snappy Tunes Recording Studio**. We're practising our brand-new song, **"Eye of the Tigershark"**.

'Come on, Finley,' says Hunter. She gives me an encouraging fins-up. 'You got it this time!'

I stick out my tongue and stretch my fins. At the end of the song is a **mad, fully sick, totes off-the-hook guitar riff.**

It starts out great.

Bow-tikka-wow-wikka YOW-YOW-YOW!

Bow-tikka-wow-wikka

YEEEEEEEEE!

Hunter, Gilleon and Gnash slam their fins over their earholes.

'YEOWCH!'

'I can't do it,' I moan. 'My fins just can't move **fast enough!**'

'You'll get it right,' says Hunter. 'Keep practising.'

Hugo, our band manager, tugs on his moustache. (It's kind of his thing.) 'We'll get it right,' he says, 'even if it takes all afternoon. Don't forget, this is your opening song at the **Rhythm and Chews festival** this weekend – it'll be the greatest song launch ever!'

'Gnash love new song,' says Gnash with a grin. 'Our best yet!'

I put down my guitar and sigh. Gnash is right. It is the **best song** I've ever written. But why did I make that final riff so complicated?!

'What if I can't pull it off?' I say. 'Everyone at the festival will laugh at me.'

Hunter
puts a fin
around my
shoulder.
'You'll do great,'
she says. 'If you
can conquer your stage fright
and sing in front of thousands of
people, then you've **definitely**
got this.'

I nod. She's right. Plus, I'd hate
to let the band down.

'Let's take a break and put
on the radio,' suggests Gilleon.
'Hearing our songs on **CHOMP
FM** always cheers me up.'

Gnash flicks on the radio.

'And that was "Achy Breaky Shark", the latest smash hit by newcomers The Killer Wails! Aren't they KILLER-RIFFIC?'

'Another smash hit?' says Hunter. 'The Killer Wails have been topping the charts all month!'

'I heard their last concert sold out in eight seconds,' says Gill.

142

'I heard **Steven Eelberg** is making a movie about them,' I say. 'Gnash hear Killer Wails are **robots** programmed to take over **Chumville,**' says Gnash.

Hunter rolls her eyes. 'That's **sea-donk-ulous,**' she says. 'But still...they've only been on the air for a few weeks. How are they so popular already?'

'Can't quite put my fin on it...'

'There's something weird about their songs, too,' I say, tapping my chin. 'They're kind of... **familiar**.'

'Well, you'll get a good chance to scope them out at **Rhythm and Chews**,' says Hugo. 'They're scheduled to play right before you. Now, let's get back to rehearsals. We've got a song to launch!'

2

Chapter Two

The next day at school I can barely keep my eyes open. Hugo made me stay back late and practise the riff in our new song **a hundred and fifty times.**

It didn't go very well.

OWCH!

**Fins stuck
in strings**

Guitar caught fire

Attracted a swarm of jellyfish

Conjured a demon

'Who disturbs SHARKLOR? Don't you know it's TACO night!'

Hunter, Gnash, Gilleon and I toss our bags into our lockers.

'Hey, isn't that **Shelley Newfins?**' says Hunter.

'Doesn't she usually wear a **JAWSOME** T-shirt?' I say.

KILLER-RIFFIC!

'Orca really isn't her colour,' sniffs Gilleon.

Gnash and I swap a worried look. 'First, The Killer Wails are all over the radio,' I say. 'And now *this*?'

Hunter shrugs. 'So what? Shelley can like other music. We have plenty more **fans in the sea.**'

We head off to our classroom and sail inside. My heart sinks a little. Hunter's wrong – it's not only Shelley Newfins. *Everyone* is wearing The Killer Wails T-shirts. Even Mr Rodney!

And that's only the beginning. All day, kids listen to The Killer Wails on their **shell-phones**.

They talk about The Killer Wails in class.

Some even do their **school projects** on them.

Things get **TOTES crazy** when **Mrs Prune**, the school gardener, swims past the classroom window.

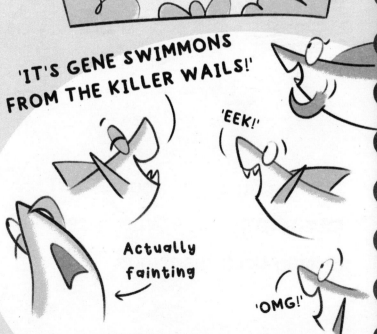

At lunch, the four of us sit at our table, feeling miserable.

I heave a deep sigh. 'What are we gonna do?' I moan. 'We're **losing fans** by the second!'

'I don't get it,' says Hunter. 'It took us **years** to build a fan base.'

'Come on, guys, you're **over-reacting!**' says Gilleon, tossing tossing back his fringe.

'We're **JAWSOME!** We've got six hundred krillion fans, remember?'

'I guess,' I say slowly. 'And we are headlining tomorrow's festival.'

'And don't forget about the ribbon-cutting for the new **Town Square** on Monday,' Gilleon adds.

Gnash whips out a giant pair of scissors.
'Yup!
Been
practising.'

Hunter scratches her chin, looking worried. 'I don't know,' she says slowly. 'If we want to stay **number one**, we better bring our **A-game** tomorrow. Which means, Finley, whatever happens, you're gonna have to nail that riff. The fate of Jawsome **depends on it!'**

Chapter Three

When I wake up on Saturday morning, I feel sick in my guts.

Today is the **Rhythm and Chews festival.**

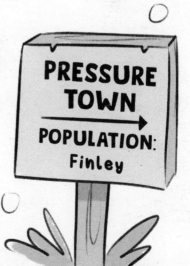

PRESSURE TOWN →

POPULATION: Finley

All the biggest names will be there, like **The Squid Laroi, Shoalivia Rodrigo**, even retro sharks like **MC Hammerhead**.

And The Killer Wails, of course.

I nervously tug on my **leather jacket** and **dark sunglasses**. When I look in the mirror, **Felix Frenzy** looks back.

Felix is **cool**.
Calm.
A **reel rock star**.
But inside, I'm still Finley.
Small. Shy. And right now...
a total scaredy-fish.

If I don't get that riff just perfect, our new song will be a flop. And that could be the end of everything. No more shows. No more albums. **No more Jawsome!**

The tour sub picks me up at 8am and takes us all to the **Chumville Showgrounds**.

FIN-PAINTING

We drive through the gates, whizzing past the giant ball pit, the chum smoothie stands, the food tents and the fin-painting booth.

Out the window I can see the crowds already milling about in front of the stages, trying to get a good spot.

We park up the back with the other bands.

By now I'm so nervous, my **fins are shaking** as I tune up my guitar. I'm so sweaty, the stage assistant can't even put my stage make-up on. In warm-up, my vocals are so tight I sound like a **freshly hatched seagull**.

Finally, it's time to go on stage. Hugo waves encouragingly from the wings. I hover behind the microphone, my guitar clutched in my fins.

This *is* it.

Our big chance!

I can't mess it up.

The curtain rises and I hold my breath. Gnash taps out a steady drum roll. Gill lets out a few chords on the keyboard, and Hunter brings in the bass.

And a one, and a two, and a...

The Showgrounds come into view.

Hunter, Gnash, Gilleon and I **all**

gasp. Our instruments fall silent.

What we see before us is a

COMPLETE
CRAB-TASTROPHE.

4

Chapter Four

The entire field in front of the
stage is...

...empty.

No one

Nada

Totes
shark-free!

Well. **Almost**. One old shark hovers in the middle of the field. He has a cane and thick glasses and looks a bit lost.

'Woo!' he shouts. 'It's **Seal Diamond!**'

'Hey!' cries Gill, his fins on his hips. 'We're not Seal Diamond. We're **JAWSOME!**'

'Who?' rasps the old shark.

'Jawsome!' Hunter shouts back.

'Jordan?'

'JAWSOME!'

'Boresome?'

'JAWSOME!'

'Eh?'

The old shark glares at us. 'Boooo! I want Seal Diamond!'

Hugo quickly drops the curtain back down.

'What happened?' asks Hunter as we all crowd around Hugo. 'Did we get the time wrong?'

'Did everyone get food poisoning from the food tents?' I ask.

'Abducted by aliens?' says Gnash.

Hugo whips out the program. 'No, you're definitely supposed to be on now,' he says, scratching his head.

Then his moustache droops. 'Oh, no…'

'What?' I ask, my heart sinking.

This does not sound good.

'Er – looks like I read the program wrong,' he says. 'The Killer Wails aren't on before you. They're on at the **same time,** over on the **Stingray Stage**. I guess everyone must be over at their show.'

I can hardly believe it. The Killer Wails stole our **entire audience?!**

'B-b-but we're **JAWSOME!'** moans Gill. '600 krillion fans! Three Gold albums! Eleven #1 hits on Chomp FM!'

'We've never had an empty crowd before,' sniffs Hunter. 'EVER!'

Gnash's bottom lip starts to tremble. **'J—J—Jawsome**… not famous anymore?'

Hunter, Gilleon and Gnash burst into tears, falling into a group hug.

As for me…

I am disappointed. All the way down to my fins.

But...part of me is also a tiny bit happy. If our show is cancelled, I'll have more time to practise that **impossible riff**.

'YES! I mean, oh no...'

Phew.

While I pretend to look as sad as the others, Hugo gets a phone call. When he comes back, his moustache is droopier than ever.

'That was the Mayor's office,' he says. 'They've **cancelled** your ribbon-cutting at the new Town Square.'

Hunter puts her fins on her hips. 'Let me guess. They want The Killer Wails to do it instead?'

'Yep,' says Hugo. He looks **turtley crushed**. 'Sorry, team.'

Gill blows into his handkerchief. I haven't seen him look this upset since they cancelled his favourite TV show, **Beverly Shells 90210**.

'If we don't figure out how to get back in the spotlight,' he wails, 'Jawsome might be toast **forever!**'

While Hugo and our roadies pack up our gear, we take off our leather jackets and sunglasses and sail over to the food tents for a chum smoothie. Sharks sail past, barely glancing at us. Without our **stage costumes,** we're just regular grade four kids.

'This is the worst day in Jawsome's history,' says Hunter morosely. 'I hate to think what all the newspapers will say tomorrow.'

As we slurp our chum smoothies, **Shelley Newfins** from school sails past.

She sees us by the smoothie stand and comes over.

'Hey, guys! Did you catch The Killer Wail's show? They're giving out whale-loads of merch for FREE! **KILLER-RIFFIC!**'

Before we can answer she scoots off towards the porta-loos, chanting, **'Killer-riffic! Killer-riffic!'**

'Honking hermit crabs,' says Gilleon. 'Why didn't we think of giving out free merch?'

'Merch, smerch,' shrugs Hunter. 'Once we release our new song on **CHOMP FM,** we'll be right on top again. Right, Finley?'

I gulp. 'Er – right!'

Looks like I'm not off the hook after all.

'I mean, come on, guys,' says Hunter, a gleam in her eye. 'We can totes **turn this around**. Besides,' she adds with a sigh, 'it's not like it could get any worse!'

Chapter Five

It gets worse.

WAY worse.

On **Sunday,** Hugo calls us to tell us all of our upcoming gigs have been

cancelled.

On **Monday,** all the shops in town ditch our music for **The Killer Wails'** new album:

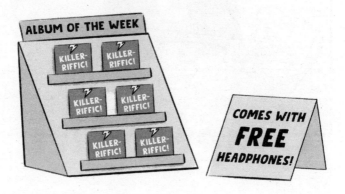

Then on **Tuesday**...

But **Friday** is the WORST:

'So what now?' says Gilleon.
Even his fringe looks sad.

'I guess we go back to being
regular kids,' I say with a shrug.

'No more concerts,' sighs Hunter.
'No more VIP lounges and
celebrity interviews.'

'No more tour bus,' says Gilleon
with a sniffle. 'I'm really going to
miss that **jaw-cuzzi.**'

'Not all bad news,' says Gnash.
'Still have us. Friends forever,
JAWSOME or no **JAWSOME!**'

I smile at Gnash. 'You're right, buddy,' I say. 'No one can take that away.'

Even though Gnash makes a good point, I'm feeling **miserable as a blobfish** when I sail into school the following Monday.

Miserable

Blobfish: officially the saddest fish alive

Totes glum

Local fish wins lotto prize of a bazillion dollars

BREAKING NEWS!

I find Hunter, Gilleon and Gnash
hanging out by the tuckshop.
Hunter is gnawing on a table.

'What's wrong?' I ask her as I
sit down. 'Why aren't you eating
something from the tuckshop?'

Nom nom nom

'It's closed,' she says through a
mouthful of wood.

'Munch 'n' Crunch Larry not
here today,' explains Gnash.

'Oh.' I look around and frown. It's not only Munch 'n' Crunch Larry who isn't here. The **entire schoolyard** is empty.

No one on the sea-monkey bars.

No cool kids by the fin-ball courts.

Not even anyone lined up at the loo block.

'Er…it is a school day, right?' I ask the others.

Hunter flips open her diary – or what's left of it, anyway. 'It's definitely Monday,' she says.

'**School holidays?**' says Gill.

'Not yet.'

'**Fish-mas?**' says Gnash.

'Nope. That's next month.'

Gnash looks sad. 'Oh. Gnash love **Santa Jaws.**'

'Maybe everyone's at home with **lobsterpox?**' suggests Gilleon.

'There was a big outbreak over in **Oysterville** last week.'

'Yeah, that's gotta be it,' I say, looking around the playground. I can't help but shiver. I've never seen our schoolyard so quiet. It's **otterly creepy**.

The bell rings and we all swim over to our classroom.

There's no one there, either.

'Okay, something **sea-spicious** is definitely going on,' says Gill. 'No students, and now no teachers. This is more bizarre than an episode of **Stranger Fins!**'

We sail around the school, checking every classroom. We check the **library,** the **teachers' lounge**, the **gym. All empty!**

The last place we check is the **principal's office.**

'Look!' gasps Gilleon. 'Someone's inside.'

He's right. My shoulders sag with relief. Principal Flotsam is sitting at his desk, looking at his computer screen.

We **bust** through the door.

'Principal Flotsam!' shouts
Hunter. 'There's an emergency!
The entire school is deserted...'

She trails off as the principal's
chair slowly turns to face us.
We all gasp.

Principal Flotsam's eyes roll back in his head. Drool spills from his jaws. **'Guuh,'** he moans, waving his fins. It's like he can't even see us!

'Oh, no!' cries Hunter. 'Principal Flotsam has been turned into a...

Z-Z-ZOMBIE!'

Chapter Six

'**SWIM!**' cries Gilleon.

We shoot out of the principal's office and **zoom** through the admin building.

'What now?' I ask, looking around as we burst through the main doors. My fins are trembling so bad I think they might fall off.

Guuuuh

'Let's go into town,' suggests Hunter, looking as scared as I feel. 'Maybe we can find a police officer.'

When we get there, a shiver snakes down my spine. Just like our school, the streets are **completely empty**.

Suddenly we hear something coming from uptown.

We wait nervously in the middle of the empty road, our **tailfins shaking**.

198

Then we see it – a **giant crowd** of sharks, coming up over the rise.

'Look!' shouts Gill in delight. 'Everyone's back! See? They were all probably getting pedicures at the mall or something.'

'The **whole town?**' says Hunter, looking doubtful.

Gnash gasps. 'Uh-oh,' he says. 'Them not sharks. Them **Z-Z-ZOMBIES!**'

Gnash is right.

Marching towards us is the **entire town of Chumville**. And every single shark has been turned into a **ZOMBIE,** just like Principal Flotsam!

At the front is Mayor Dorsaldoff, **groaning** and **moaning**. Behind him is Mr Rodney, then Dim Wittleson, our school bully.

Then my mum and dad, and all my brothers and sisters. Even my pet prawn, Justin, has been **zombiefied**.

It's a total

ZOMBIE–POCALYPSE.

Then Hunter frowns. 'Has anyone noticed anything **weird** about these zombies?' she asks.

'Their moans are super **off-key?**' says Gill.

'They're not trying to **eat our brains?**' I suggest.

'Not paying **parking fees?**' says Gnash.

'No, not that,' says Hunter. 'They're all wearing headphones. And not just any headphones... **Killer Wails' headphones.**'

We look around. Hunter's right! Even Justin is wearing teeny little headphones. (They are **SO cute**.

Come on, Finley, focus!)

'Hey, check this out!' I zoom towards an electronics store.

'The Killer Wails are on **every channel.**'

Gill frowns. 'Wait, isn't that the same **music video** Principal Flotsam was watching?'

'You're right,' I say. 'But why can't **we** hear anything?'

Hunter looks from the screens to the zombie sharks behind them, her eyes narrowed. Then she gasps. 'Of course,' she says, 'it's the **headphones**. The Killer Wails must be transmitting their songs directly to them, and somehow it's turning everyone into **mindless zombies!**'

'But **how?**' I say.

'**Music frequencies,**' says Gnash.

Hunter's eyes light up. 'That's it, Gnash! Music is broadcast using certain frequencies. The Killer Wails must have altered the **radio signals!**'

'So instead of sending out music,' says Gill, 'they're sending out radio signals that hijack **brain waves?** Ew!'

Hunter nods. 'Which means right now we're the **only sharks** in Chumville who aren't under their **mind control.**'

'**Brain waves** and **mind control**...' I muse. 'Just what are The Killer Wails up to?'

Gilleon peers closer at one of the TV screens. 'Wait a second... this is a **live recording,**' he says. 'And it's coming from **Snappy Tunes Recording Studio.**'

'Come on!' says Hunter, getting

a gleam in her eye. She starts
swimming towards **Cray Mart**.
'We've got to get to the studio and
end that transmission. But first,'
she adds, 'we're gonna need some
earmuffs.'

Chapter Seven

Ten minutes later we're **high-tailing** it towards Snappy Tunes Recording Studio.

'Are you sure these are going to protect us from the **mind control?'**

I ask Hunter.

'**Ab-sea-lutely,**' says Hunter.
'If these things can block out my
mum's snoring, they can block
out mind control waves.'

'And what's Gnash's deal?' I ask.

'Yeah,' scowls Gill. 'He's
cramping my style.'

Hunter shrugs. 'I couldn't find earmuffs big enough. Come on, we can sneak in through the back entrance.'

We follow Hunter around the back of the recording studio. All studios have a **secret back entrance,** in case there are too many fans out front.

STEP ONE: Enter top secret door code

STEP TWO: Pass retina scanner

'Scanning...
Welcome,
Felix Frenzy!'

STEP THREE: Cross lava pit

STEP FOUR: Answer a dragon's riddle

Once inside, we head for the downstairs recording studio, where we're stopped by...

'Hugo!' we all cry.

'Guuuuuh,' moans Hugo.

'Oh, no,' I say. 'Hugo's been zombiefied too!'

'Paasswooord,' Hugo groans.

'Huh?' says Gill.

'Wrooong,' moans Hugo.

Hunter's eyes light up. 'He's asking for a password,' she says.

'**Wrooong!**' Hugo shouts. He's starting to look angry.

We all swap a look, thinking hard. A password...

I look at Hugo's **T-shirt** and it hits me.

'**Killer-riffic!**' I cry.

Hugo groans and lumbers aside.

'**Corrrrrreeeeect.**'

'Let's sneak in,' says Hunter. 'Orcas are super strong fighters. And watch your nostrils – their slow digestive system makes them smell super bad.'

She carefully pushes the door open and we duck inside the studio, diving behind a couch.

Thankfully, The Killer Wails don't seem to notice us – they're  too busy putting on their show for the cameras.

I frown.

'I thought you said orcas **smell bad,**' I say. 'I can't smell anything.'

Hunter sniffs the water. 'Weird.

Me neither,' she says. 'All I can smell is **soy chum-a-latte** and…mmm, **jellyfish doughnuts!**' She smacks her lips. 'I'm *starving*.'

'Hunter,' I whisper back, 'you're *always* starving.'

Beside me, Gilleon's hips start to sway. His shoulders jiggle and his tailfin taps out a beat.

'Gilleon,' Hunter hisses. 'What are you doing?! Put your **earmuffs** back on!'

'I can't help it!' he says, bopping his head along to the music. 'I feel like I've heard this song

before...it's **kinda catchy!** Then his eyes go blank. His jaw goes slack, and he starts to drool. **'Guh,'** he groans. **'Uuuuuuunnngh.'**

'Oh, no!' I whisper. **'He's going zombie!'**

Hunter grabs Gilleon's earmuffs and shoves them back over his head. 'Snap out of it, Gill!' she says.

I wave my fin in front of his face. Nothing.

'Gnash have idea,' says Gnash. He lifts up one of Gill's earmuffs and says, **'Cosmopolifin magazine** say stripes and spots hot new look!'

Gilleon's face pales. His eyes bulge. But he does stop drooling. 'Cosmo said **WHAT?!**' he cries.

'Good thinking, Gnash,' says Hunter. 'Nothing scares Gilleon like a fashion disaster.'

'Looks like you were right,' I say to Hunter. 'Their **music** is putting everyone under some kind of **spell!**'

'Exactly,' says Hunter. 'Now we just need to figure out how to stop it.'

'Can't we switch it off?' says Gill.

'But how do we shut off an entire studio broadcast?' I ask.

'Just pull plug,' says Gnash with a shrug.

'**Krilliant idea,** Gnash!' grins Hunter. She looks over at the mixing board. It's full of **wires** and **knobs** and **dials**. 'Hmm,' she says. 'Hugo normally handles all of this **techy stuff**. Which plug do we pull?'

'Not there,' says Gnash, pointing at the wall behind The Killer Wails. '*Those plugs.*'

We all look over to where Gnash is pointing. Four cords snake out from their power points.

'Wait a second!' gasps Hunter.

'Those aren't real orcas,' I say, 'th-th-they're… **ROBOTS!**'

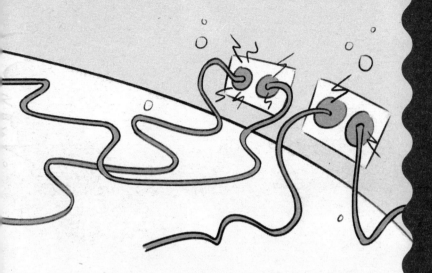

'No wonder they're not smelly,' says Gilleon. 'Robots don't even have **digestive systems!**'

'We better pull those plugs, and quick!' I cry.

Hunter thinks for a moment. 'You're right, Finley,' she says. 'And you're **JUST the shark to do it.**'

Chapter Eight

'M-m-me?' I squeak.

Hunter nods.

'You're **small** and **fast** and they might not see you.'

'Might not?' I whine.

'What if they do?'

'We'll jump in and **save your fins,** of course,' says Gill.

I sigh. Hunter's right. I am small and fast. 'Fine.'

Making sure my earmuffs are secure, I sneak over to the edge of the couch. The Killer Wails are facing the other way, performing into the cameras. My tailfin trembles nervously as I sail over to the power point on the wall. With a shaking fin, I tug the plugs free one by one.

Thok!   Thok!

Thok!   Thok!

Wrrrrrrr...

Behind me, The Killer Wails
wind down, their fins dropping,
faces frozen mid-song.

I carefully remove my earmuffs.
Sweet silence.
We did it!

I turn and give Hunter, Gilleon
and Gnash a quick fins up.

They all grin back at me.

Then their grins **disappear**.

A shadow falls over me and I
look up – all four of The Killer
Wails are hovering above me,
their faces turned to mean scowls.

'Get out of there, Finley!' Hunter
cries. 'They must have a **back-
up power source!'**

I zoom over to my friends as
fast as I can. Hunter jets ahead

and opens the door. 'Everyone
SWIM!' she cries.

We all hightail it through the
door, whizzing past Hugo and out
of the studio. I toss a look behind
me. The Killer Wails are **right
on our tailfins!**

We race towards town.

Hunter points to a **billboard** up ahead. 'Quick! We can hide there.'

Once they're gone, we all sigh with relief. 'It's time to take those evil robots down,' says Hunter.

'How do we do that?' asks Gill.

Hunter thinks for a moment. I can almost see her big brain working. 'If The Killer Wails are using **sound frequencies** to control the town...maybe we can undo it with a **different** sound. All we need is a stage, a microphone and some speakers.' Then her eyes light up and she points towards the centre of town. 'To **Town Square!**'

Chapter Nine

We carefully weave our way through town, keeping an eye out for The Killer Wails.

We're almost at **City Hall** when Hunter gasps and herds us all behind a bus stop.

'Oh, no!' she moans. 'One of them is keeping guard at the Main Street crossing.'

'How do we get past?' I ask shakily.

'We'll have to blend in,' says Hunter. 'There's loads of zombies out there – just hold out your fins and groan.'

Gilleon lets out a huff. 'I do not **"blend in",** he says. 'It's against the **diva code.'**

'Just pretend you're starring

in the **Kriller** video,' suggests Hunter. 'You know, that famous zombie song by **Michael Jackfin?'**

Gill's eyes light up. **'SLAY!'**

Striking our best zombie poses, we slip into the crowd and cross the street.

Hnghghghg

I watch the orca robot as we pass, making my face extra drooly. **'Gilleon,'** Hunter hisses. 'Less dancing, more groaning.' Finally we get to the other side, unnoticed. Hunter leads us over to City Hall. Out the front is **Town Square**.

'Fin-tastic!' grins Hunter. 'It's still set up for the **opening ceremony.'**

236

'Gnash cut ribbon?' Gnash asks excitedly, pulling out his **giant scissors**.

I pat him on the back. 'Not today, buddy,' I say. 'Maybe next time.'

Hunter zips around the square, checking the equipment. 'These speakers are **ginormous!** We can put on a show the entire town will hear. Our **new song** is bound to snap everyone back to reality.'

I gasp. My tailfin starts to tremble again. 'You want us to play our **new** song?' I squeal.

Oh, no.

'Aren't you forgetting something, Hunter?' Gilleon says. 'We have no **instruments**.'

Hunter looks around the square with that good old gleam in her eye. 'Let me handle that.'

Hunter drops a drum kit, two guitars and a keyboard in front of us.

'Er…no drumsticks?' says Gnash.

'No problem,' says Hunter. 'I think I **swallowed some** this morning.'

rattle
rattle

Only slightly drooly

'Here you go!'

Hunter pushes Gilleon and Gnash onto the stage. 'Come on, Finley!' she cries.

I nervously hover behind one of the giant speakers. 'I c-c-can't,' I stammer. She rushes down to drag me up onto the stage. **'I'm not ready!'**

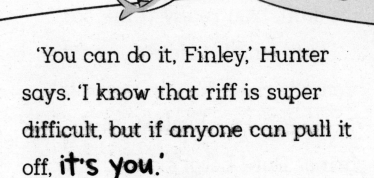

'You can do it, Finley,' Hunter says. 'I know that riff is super difficult, but if anyone can pull it off, **it's you.'**

A lump starts to form in my throat. Hunter's wrong. I've tried and tried, but it's **otterly fin-possible**. 'Can't we sing one of our old songs instead?' I ask.

Hunter looks around. 'Everyone already knows those songs. We need something new. And it really is the best song you've ever written – maybe even the best song **anyone's** ever written!'

I sniff. 'You really think so?'

Hunter nods. 'Listen…maybe you are right. Maybe that riff is too hard for **Finley.**' She grins. 'But I bet it's a total cinch for **Felix Frenzy.'**

The lump in my throat goes away. Hunter's right. Felix Frenzy can do **anything**.

'Okay,' I say shakily, then I take up position at the microphone, ready to put on our **best show ever.**

Chapter Ten

As soon as we strike our first chord, I know Hunter's plan is **genius**.

The speakers are so loud that every shark in Town Square turns our way.

First, they take off their **headphones**.

Next, their **heads** begin to **nod**. Then their **tailfins** start to **swing**. Their fins swish, **floosh-floosh-floosh** to the beat.

Shoulders **jiggle,** hips **wiggle**.

Fins are thrown up over heads, and sharks are **jiving** and **spinning** and **dancing** like

I've never seen before.

Hugo was right. This really IS our **best song ever!**

Soon, more sharks arrive, drawn by the music. Hunter turns the volume up even louder, and within seconds the square is packed. I try not to think about the riff as we groove through the song.

247

'It's working!' Gilleon cries, beaming at the crowd. 'They're **un-zombiefying!**'

'Uh-oh,' says Gnash, pointing a drumstick at the horizon. Coming over the rise are four orcas – The Killer Wails.

'Don't get distracted,' shouts Hunter. 'Keep playing!'

I look around. Gill's right – it **is** working. Everyone in the crowd is blinking and rubbing

their eyes. The mind control is wearing off!

At that moment The Killer Wails storm into Town Square, barrelling towards us.

'Louder!' cries Hunter, turning the speakers up to eleven. 'Let's **fry their circuits!**'

We smash the chorus, and then it's time. *The impossible riff.*

I take a deep breath and remember what Hunter said. Impossible for **Finley,** maybe. But easy-peasy for a **rock star** like Felix Frenzy. **And I am Felix Frenzy!** I let my fins take over. Instead of thinking about the riff, I **feel the music**.

I smash it! My fins move like lightning! Smoke rises from my guitar, but I don't dare to stop.

The crowd **goes wild**. I play even faster. It's easy. It's fun. It's **not impossible** at all!

Blue sparks start to spit from The Killer Wails. Their heads spin like possessed demons, and their jaws fly right off. Finally they collapse on the ground, **broken** and **twitching**.

'WE DID IT!' cries Hunter as the song hits its final note.

I lower my guitar, a **giant grin** stretching across my face. I did it! **I nailed the riff!**

Down in the crowd, sharks clap and cheer. Free from The Killer Wails' mind control, they hug and high-fin each other.

'**JAWSOME** save Chumville!' shouts Gnash. 'Hooray!' He pulls us into a group hug.

Suddenly Hunter pulls free, sniffing the water. 'There's that smell again,' she says. '**Soy chum-a-latte** and **jellyfish doughnuts**. It can't be...'

She heads for a patch of seaweed at the edge of the crowd.

Reaching in, she pulls out a shark holding a **remote control**.

We all sail over.

'Well, well, well,' Hunter says. **'Look who we have here!'**

The shark with the remote control looks sheepish. My jaw drops. I'd recognise that mullet in a heartbeat. The shark holding the remote control is

none
other
than...

Chapter Eleven

ANN CHOVI,
Jawsome's old lead
singer!

A pair of police
sharks swim our way.
'What's going on here?'
one of them asks.

Hunter grabs the remote control and presses some buttons on it. One of the orca robots twitches. 'So YOU were behind The Killer Wails and their mind-control!' she says to Ann Chovi.

'That's right, it was me,' says Ann. 'And I would have gotten away with it, too, if it wasn't for you and your **giant tiger shark brain.**'

'So that's why The Killer Wails' music was familiar,' I say. 'They're **Ann Chovi's** songs!'

'But why control Chumville?' asks Gnash.

Gilleon tosses back his fringe. 'Don't any of you watch TV? Ann got kicked off **I'm a Shell-ebrity, Get Me Trout of Here** and lost her spot on **I Wanna Be a Pop Shark** after yelling at the contestants. I guess the only way she could be famous again was to **brainwash** everyone.'

Ann Chovi glowers at him. 'I deserve to be the **number one performer** in Chumville,' she cries, 'not you **losers! JAWSOME** is nothing without me!'

'Maybe you should have thought of that before you quit our band,' says Gilleon, sticking up his nose.

'We'll take care of this,' say the officers. They put Ann Chovi in fin-cuffs and lead her away.

'Ann Chovi **super mean,**' says Gnash.

'**Good riddance,**' I add.

At that moment, Hugo finds us

and envelopes us all in a walrus-sized hug. 'You did it!' he says to me. 'You nailed the riff!'

'All thanks to Hunter,' I say, beaming at her. 'She gave me some great advice. Finley overthinks things, but **Felix...** he's **kinda unreel.'**

Hunter shakes her head. 'Oh, Finley,' she says, **'you're both unreel.** You just had to believe it was possible.'

That night, I tuck Justin into his tank and sink into my bed. It's official – **JAWSOME** are number one again. Next week, we're doing interviews at **twelve radio stations,** we have **three ribbon-cuttings,** and our new song has already gone **platinum**. Hugo's even talking about us making a **JAWSOME**

movie. **Imagine that!**

As for me...I'm ready to get some sleep. Tomorrow's another day, and nothing is ordinary when you're an internationally famous rock star. Who knows what kind of **shark-nanigans** we'll get into next?

PEACE OUT, ROCKERS!

READ MORE!

Super-professional
author photo

R.J. Timmis is an author-illustrator from the sunny Gold Coast. She loves to write magical and adventurous stories that make kids giggle. Rebecca has had lots of real-life adventures, like almost falling off the Great Wall of China, hiding from grizzly bears in Canada and being chased by wild pigs in outback Queensland. Her other jobs include coding websites, writing for the video game industry, and raising three (mostly) lovely boys.